SCRAPBOOKING with Lizzie McGuire

LIFE'S GREATEST MOMENTS ALL IN ONE BOOK... IT'S LIKE MY DIARY WITH PICTURES!

Editor: Carol Field Dahlstrom
Project Editor: Paula Marshall
Writer and Project Designer: Susan M. Banker
Designer: Angie Haupert Hoogensen
Copy Chief: Terri Fredrickson
Publishing Operations Manager: Karen Schirm
Book Production Managers: Pam Kvitne, Marjorie J. Schenkelberg, Rick von Holdt, Mark Weaver
Contributing Copy Editor: Margaret Smith
Contributing Proofreaders: Julie Cahalan, Elizabeth Havey, Sara Henderson
Photographers: Meredith Photo Studio
Project Designer: Janet Petersma
Editorial Assistants: Cheryl Eckert, Karen McFadden
Edit and Design Production Coordinator: Mary Lee Gavin

Meredith® Books
Editor in Chief: Linda Raglan Cunningham
Design Director: Matt Strelecki
Managing Editor: Gregory H. Kayko
Executive Editor, Decorating and Home Design: Denise L. Caringer

Publisher: James D. Blume
Executive Director, Marketing: Jeffrey Myers
Executive Director, New Business Development: Todd M. Davis
Executive Director, Sales: Ken Zagor
Director, Operations: George A. Susral
Director, Production: Douglas M. Johnston
Business Director: Jim Leonard

Vice President and General Manager: Douglas J. Guendel

Meredith Publishing Group
President, Publishing Group: Stephen M. Lacy
Vice President-Publishing Director: Bob Mate

Meredith Corporation
Chairman and Chief Executive Officer: William T. Kerr

In Memoriam: E.T. Meredith III (1933–2003)

Disney Publishing Worldwide, Inc.
Lisa Gerstel

Visit Lizzie every day at DisneyChannel.com

Library of Congress Control Number: 2003097939
ISBN: 0-696-22011-3

We welcome your comments and suggestions. Write to us at: Meredith Books, Crafts Editorial Department, 1716 Locust Street–LN120, Des Moines, IA 50309-3023. Or visit us at: meredithbooks.com

SCRAPBOOKING with Lizzie McGUiRE

CONTENTS

A Note from Lizzie
5
Lizzie Quiz
6–9
Good Ol' Mom
10–13
Hi, It's Just Me
14–17
School Is Cool
18–21
Time for a Snack
22–25
Born to Scrap
26–29
Me & Mom
30–33
The Artist in Me
34–37
Friends Rule
38–41
Awesome Headlines
42
Lizzie Photos
43–46
Other Ways to Use Your Photos!
47
My Family Rocks
48–51
Pottery 101
52–55
Time for TV
56–59
A Great Hair Day
60–63
School Rules!
64–67
Live Your Dream
68–71
Index
72
Lizzie Patterned Papers
73–80
Lizzie Stickers
following page 80

A Note from Lizzie!

Say, "Cheese!"

If you have photos from birthday parties, vacations, family times, hanging out with friends, and special days stashed in boxes, drawers, or your backpack, you already have the main ingredient for scrapbooking.

Cool photos show the special times you never want to forget. So get them out, sort them, and get ready to make a one-of-a-kind scrapbook that's all about you!

This book is packed with awesome ideas to help you create your scrapbooking pages. They'll be fun to make and so sweet to show off. Every group of photos is designed on three differently styled pages–you get to pick the design that suits your personality!

So come on, girlfriend, get out your scissors and glue stick–you're about to record your history.

I HAVE SO MANY COOL PHOTOS, I'M MAKING EIGHT SEPARATE SCRAPBOOKS!

How do you picture yourself today?

Being a girl is sooo cool! Some days you feel one way and sometimes another! Take this quiz and see.

#1—If I could pick my name

A. I'd stick with my own name.
B. I'd choose Annabell.
C. You could call me Zeetah.

Write down your points! A=3, B=2, C=1.

#2—My comfiest pj's are

A. T-shirt and knit shorts.
B. Flannel nightgown. (Don't tell anyone!)
C. Sweats (with socks).

Write down your points! A=3, B=1, C=2.

#3—I wear jewelry

A. Only where I'm pierced! B. Never. C. Always.

Write down your points! A=1, B=3, C=2.

#4—My favorite hairstyle is

- A. Wash and wear.
- B. A ponytail tied with a bow.
- C. Piled high, like I'm headin' for the prom.

Write down your points! A=1, B=3, C=2.

#5—My favorite shoes are

- A. None; I usually go barefoot.
- B. Lime green sneakers.
- C. Mary Janes.

Write down your points! A=1, B=2, C=3.

#6—My favorite fingernail polish is

- A. Forever Pink.
- B. Pretty and Purple with a glitter topcoat.
- C. Usually three different colors mixed until they look cool.

Write down your points! A=3, B=2 C=1.

#7—My favorite subject in school is

- A. Math.
- B. Lunch.
- C. Art.

Write down your points! A=3, B=1, C=2.

#8—I would love to travel to

- **A.** Paris, France.
- **B.** The library.
- **C.** Tasmania.

Write down your points! A=2, B=3, C=1.

#9—Talking to boys

- **A.** Makes me blush (but my friends say I look good in pink!).
- **B.** Is the highlight of my day.
- **C.** Is no big deal, they're just buddies.

Write down your points! A=1, B=2, C=3.

#10—My brother is cool

- **A.** Until he hides my makeup case.
- **B.** Except when he borrows my hair gel without asking.
- **C.** With the exception of the time he put blue food coloring in my shampoo.

Write down your points! A=3, B=2, C=1.

Seriously cool!

#11—My parents

- **A.** Rock (most of the time).
- **B.** Love me for me.
- **C.** Really need to reevaluate my allowance!

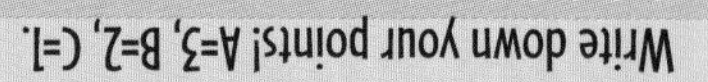

Write down your points! A=3, B=2, C=1.

#12—I love to eat

A. Pineapple Pizza. B. Burgers. C. And eat.

Write down your points! A=2, B=3, C=1.

Now total your quiz points. If they total 29-36, you are beautifully balanced!

BEAUTIFULLY BALANCED

You prefer everything organized and in place. You usually are on time and you love to wear coordinating socks and tees. You organize your photos right after you get them printed and love knowing where everything is.

If your points total 20-28, you are cool and creative!

You're full of ideas that just won't stop! You like things a little off balance—like your hair, you might wear one big ponytail on the side. You take pictures of everything even though you can't always find them after they're printed.

If your points total 12-19, you are totally off the page!

The wackier the better for you! You sleep late and you love to wear thrift shop clothes. You take photos in black and white and color them with colored pencils. You take your pet ferret with you wherever you go.

Hey, you rock even if you get a different score each time you take the quiz! It's OK to feel like a different person each day—'cause that's what's cool about being a girl! Now check out scrapbooking pages and layouts that fit your mood today and have fun scrapping!

t your vegetables. | You ca
st? | I'M Not JUST talKing t

No. | Am I talking to a brick wall? |
Don't make me tell you again. | Look at
me when I'm talking to you. | I would
have never talked to MY mother like that
| I don't care what "everyone" is doing!
Eat your vegetables. | Money doesn
grow on trees. | What would you do if
wasn't here? | You can't find it? We
where did you see it last? | I'm not ju
talking to hear myself. | Were you rais
a barn? | Act your age. | Don't use th
tone with me! | Don't run with scissors
Why? Because I said so, that's why! |
like a lady! | How about a h

Things Mothers Say...

TOTALLY OFF THE PAGE

GOOD OL' MOM

Keep a notebook handy to jot down all your mom-isms. Then include them on a clever page that spotlights the two of you.

No. | Am I talking to a brick wall? | Don't make me tell you again. | Look at me when I'm talking to you. | I would have never talked to MY mother like that! | I don't care what "everyone" is doing! | Eat your vegetables. | Money doesn't grow on trees. | What would you do if I wasn't here? | You can't find it? Well, where did you see it last? | I'm not just talking to hear myself. | Were you raised in a barn? | Act your age. | Don't use that tone with me! | Don't run with scissors. | Why? Because I said so, that's why! | Sit like a lady! |How about a hug?

Things Mothers Say...

BEAUTIFULLY BALANCED

ANOTHER GREAT IDEA!

Remember Dad too! Keep track of his favorite sayings and make a page with a photo of you two. Accent the page with stickers and die cuts of bugs, tools, cars, briefcases, or motifs about his favorite food, sport, or hobby.

Turn the page to find out how to make each of these layouts.

GOOD OL' MOM
CONTINUED

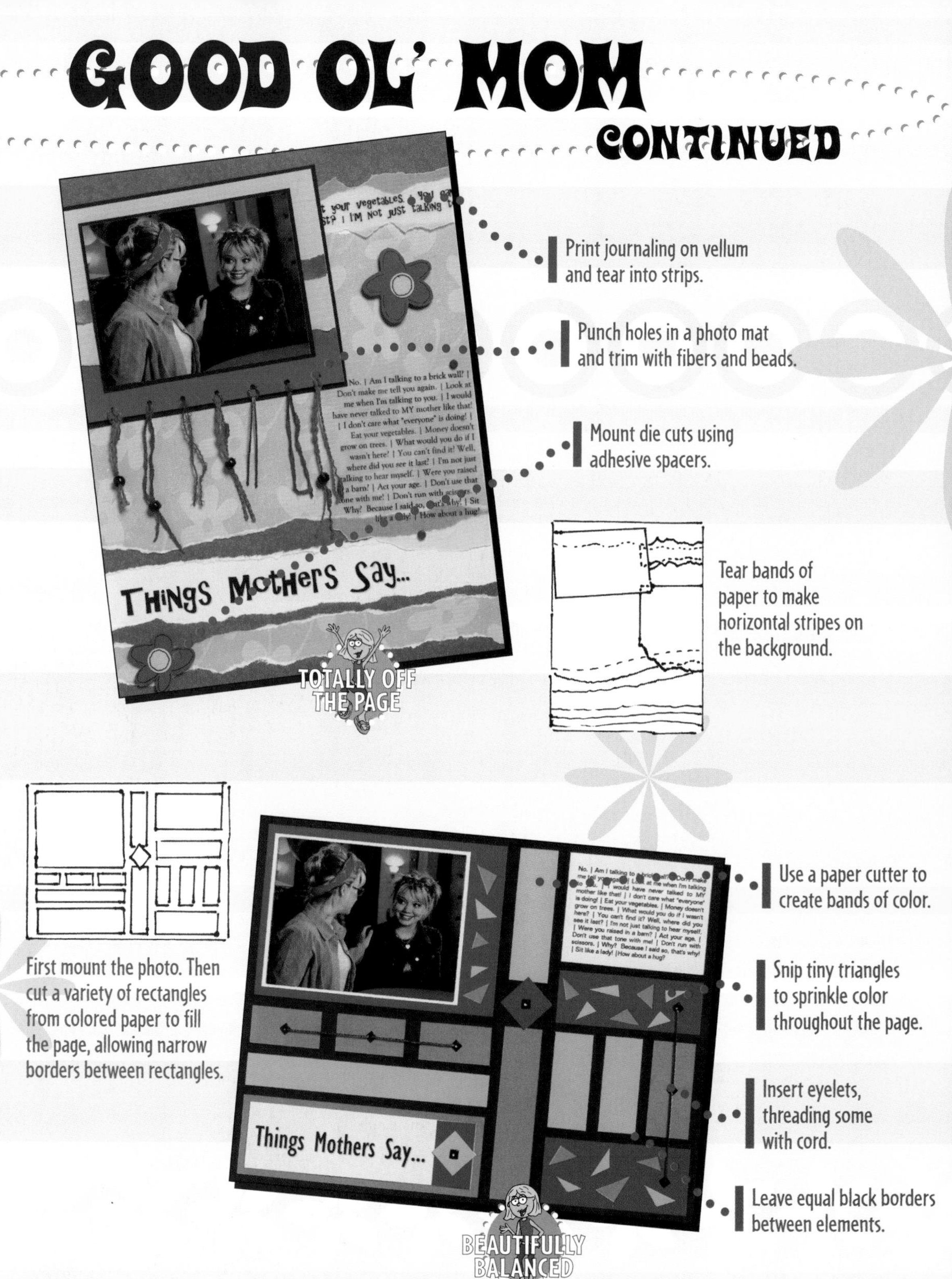

Print journaling on vellum and tear into strips.

Punch holes in a photo mat and trim with fibers and beads.

Mount die cuts using adhesive spacers.

Tear bands of paper to make horizontal stripes on the background.

First mount the photo. Then cut a variety of rectangles from colored paper to fill the page, allowing narrow borders between rectangles.

Use a paper cutter to create bands of color.

Snip tiny triangles to sprinkle color throughout the page.

Insert eyelets, threading some with cord.

Leave equal black borders between elements.

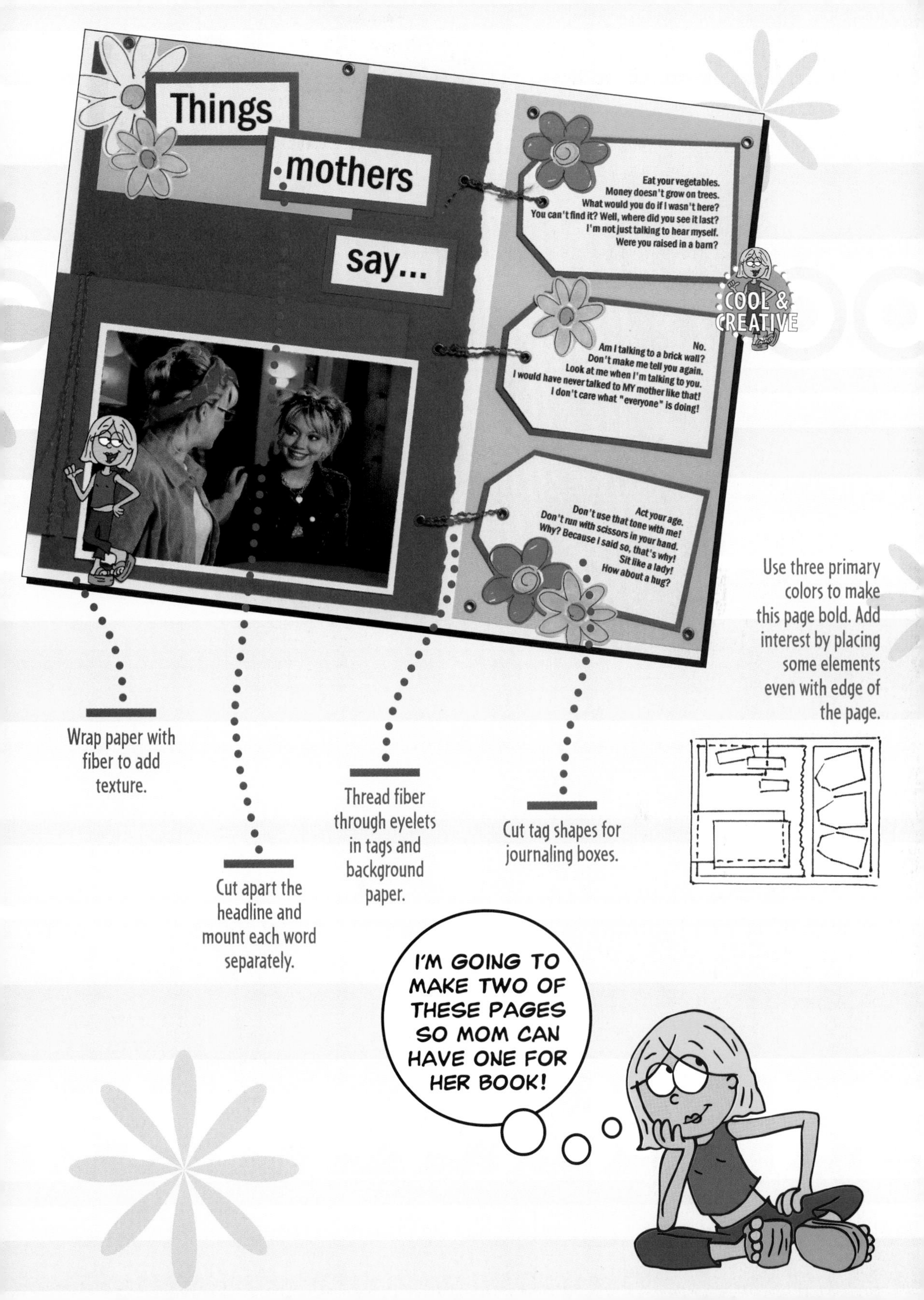

Use three primary colors to make this page bold. Add interest by placing some elements even with edge of the page.

Wrap paper with fiber to add texture.

Cut apart the headline and mount each word separately.

Thread fiber through eyelets in tags and background paper.

Cut tag shapes for journaling boxes.

caring
CURIOUS
L M
SINGER
friendly
CRAZY
SMAR
sometimes shy
D I V
outgoing
COOL
totally me
NOW
LOYAL
TOTALLY OFF THE PAGE

HI, IT'S JUST ME!

Sometimes you have a photo of yourself that for some reason you just love. Make the most of it!

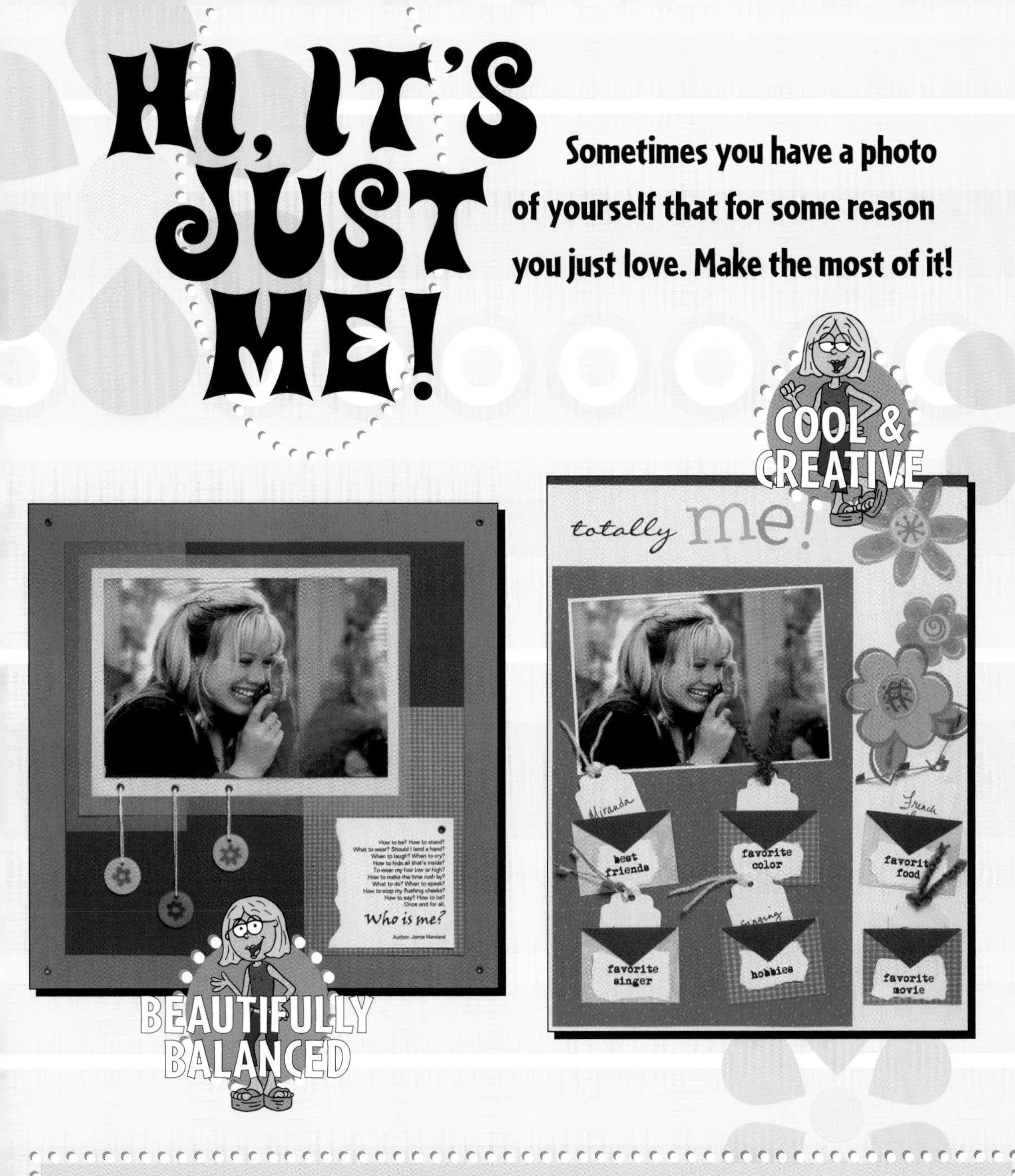

ANOTHER GREAT IDEA!

Sort photos by date, activity, or person. File the photos in an acid-free photo box. Then when you have time to scrapbook, you'll know where to find each photo. Also remember to make copies of photos if you don't want to use the original.

Turn the page to find out how to make each of these layouts.

HI, IT'S JUST ME CONTINUED

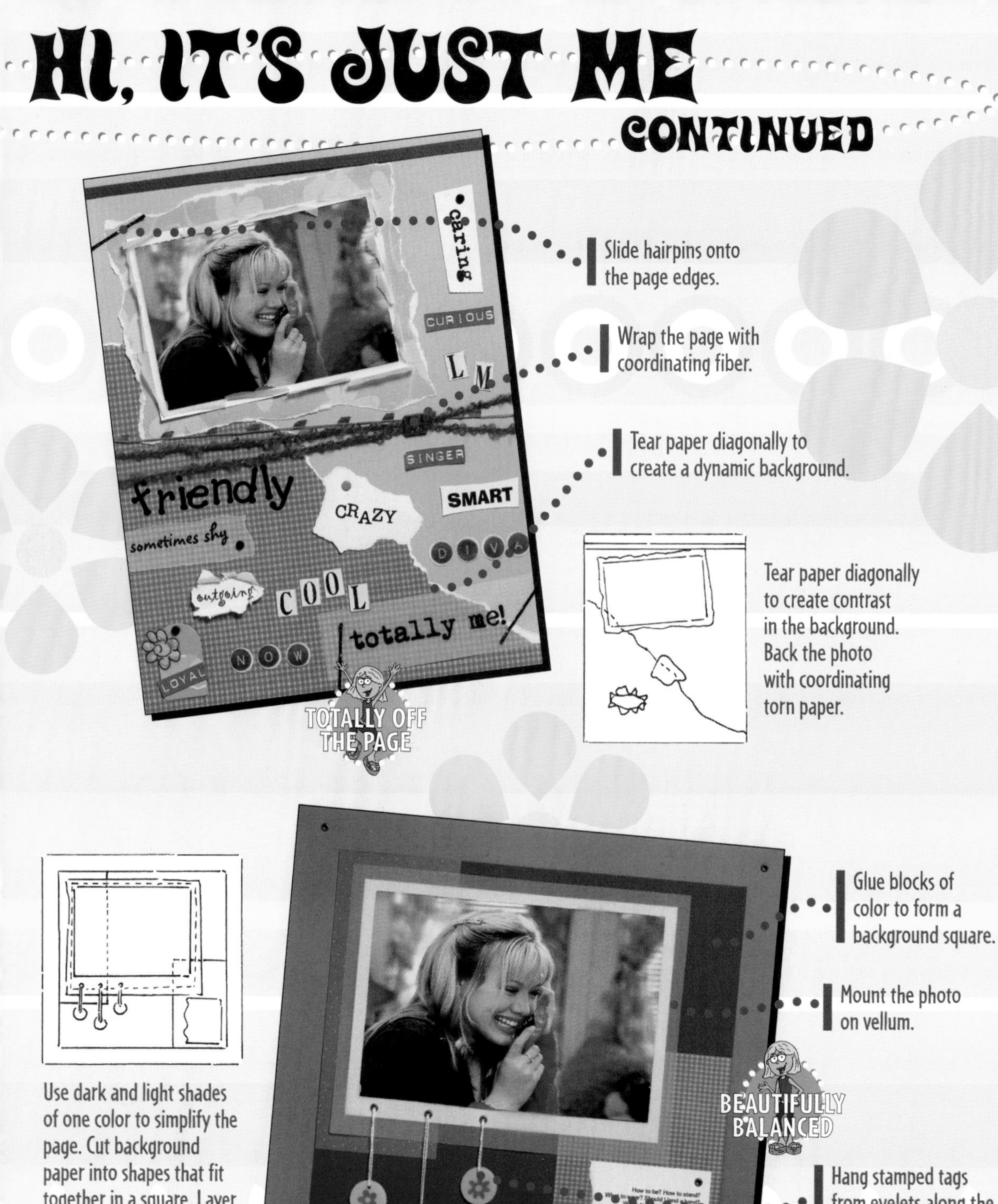

Slide hairpins onto the page edges.

Wrap the page with coordinating fiber.

Tear paper diagonally to create a dynamic background.

Tear paper diagonally to create contrast in the background. Back the photo with coordinating torn paper.

Use dark and light shades of one color to simplify the page. Cut background paper into shapes that fit together in a square. Layer smaller rectangles from light paper.

Glue blocks of color to form a background square.

Mount the photo on vellum.

Hang stamped tags from eyelets along the edge of the photo mat.

Place the headline at the bottom for a different approach.

Choose papers that coordinate with the photo. Solid or subtle patterns work best when the layout is as busy as this one.

Cut small rectangles and contrasting triangles to create the look of envelopes.

Create a headline using two styles and sizes of alphabet stickers.

Balance the page with colorful glittered stickers.

caution:
YOU ARE ABOUT TO ENTER THE
SCHOOL
Z O N E
A HAPPY
SCHOOL IS
RESPECT
WHERE YOU'LL HAVE...
DELICIOUS LUNCHES!
DEEP CONVERSATIONS!
SOCIAL ADVENTURES!
FRIENDS FOR LIFE!
L.M.
COOL & CREATIVE

SCHOOL IS COOL

There's no end to the pages you can create about school! From cheerleading to lunch, your every moment can be captured in bright pages like these!

ANOTHER GREAT IDEA!

What's your favorite part of school? Whatever it is, include it in your scrapbook. Hang on to things that will make the page, such as ticket stubs, concert programs, try-out flyers, report cards (maybe!), and other papers that show what school is all about!

Turn the page to find out how to make each of these layouts.

SCHOOL IS COOL CONTINUED

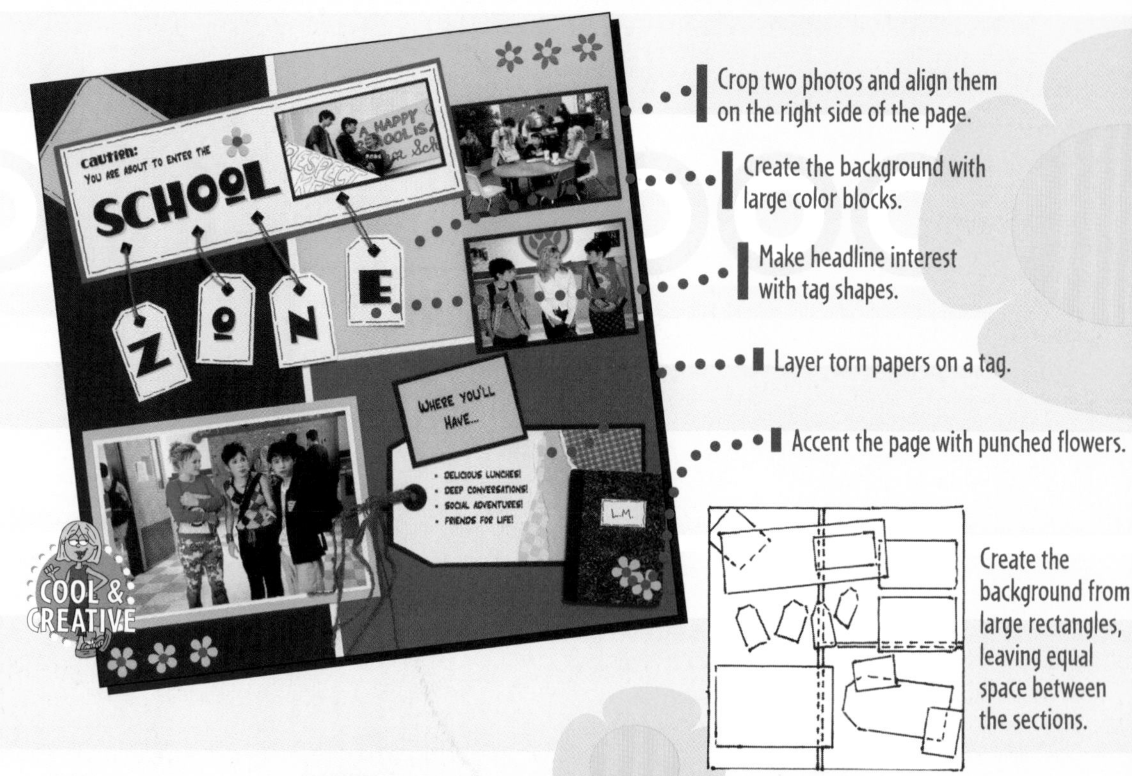

Crop two photos and align them on the right side of the page.

Create the background with large color blocks.

Make headline interest with tag shapes.

Layer torn papers on a tag.

Accent the page with punched flowers.

Create the background from large rectangles, leaving equal space between the sections.

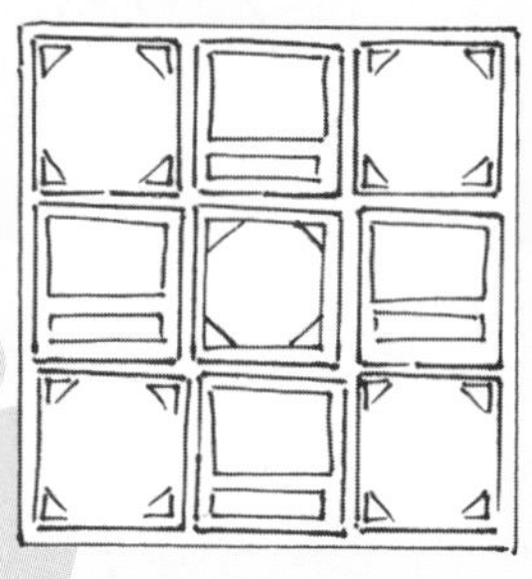

Create a gridded background by placing nine equal squares on black, making narrow borders.

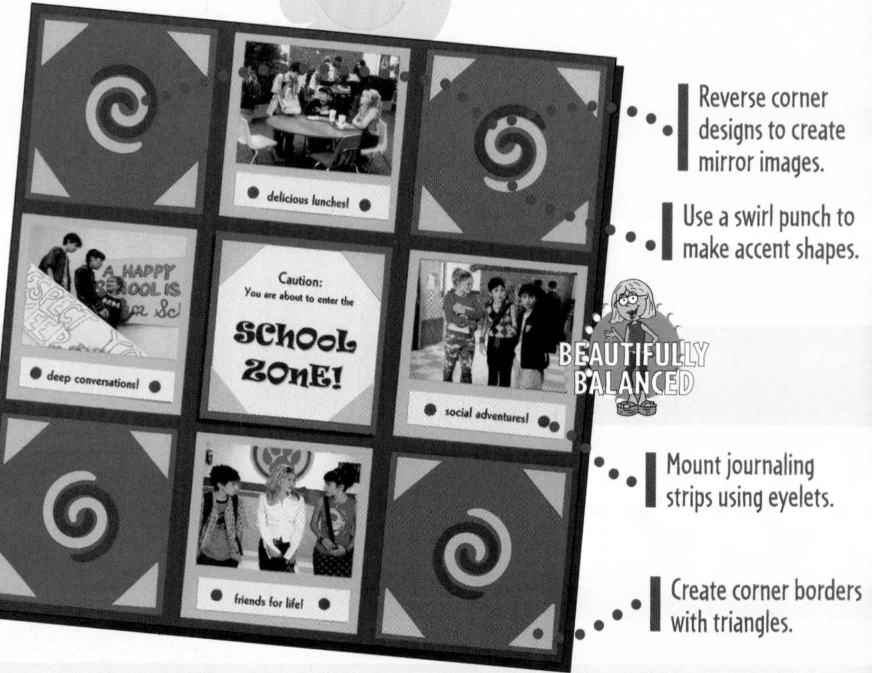

Reverse corner designs to create mirror images.

Use a swirl punch to make accent shapes.

Mount journaling strips using eyelets.

Create corner borders with triangles.

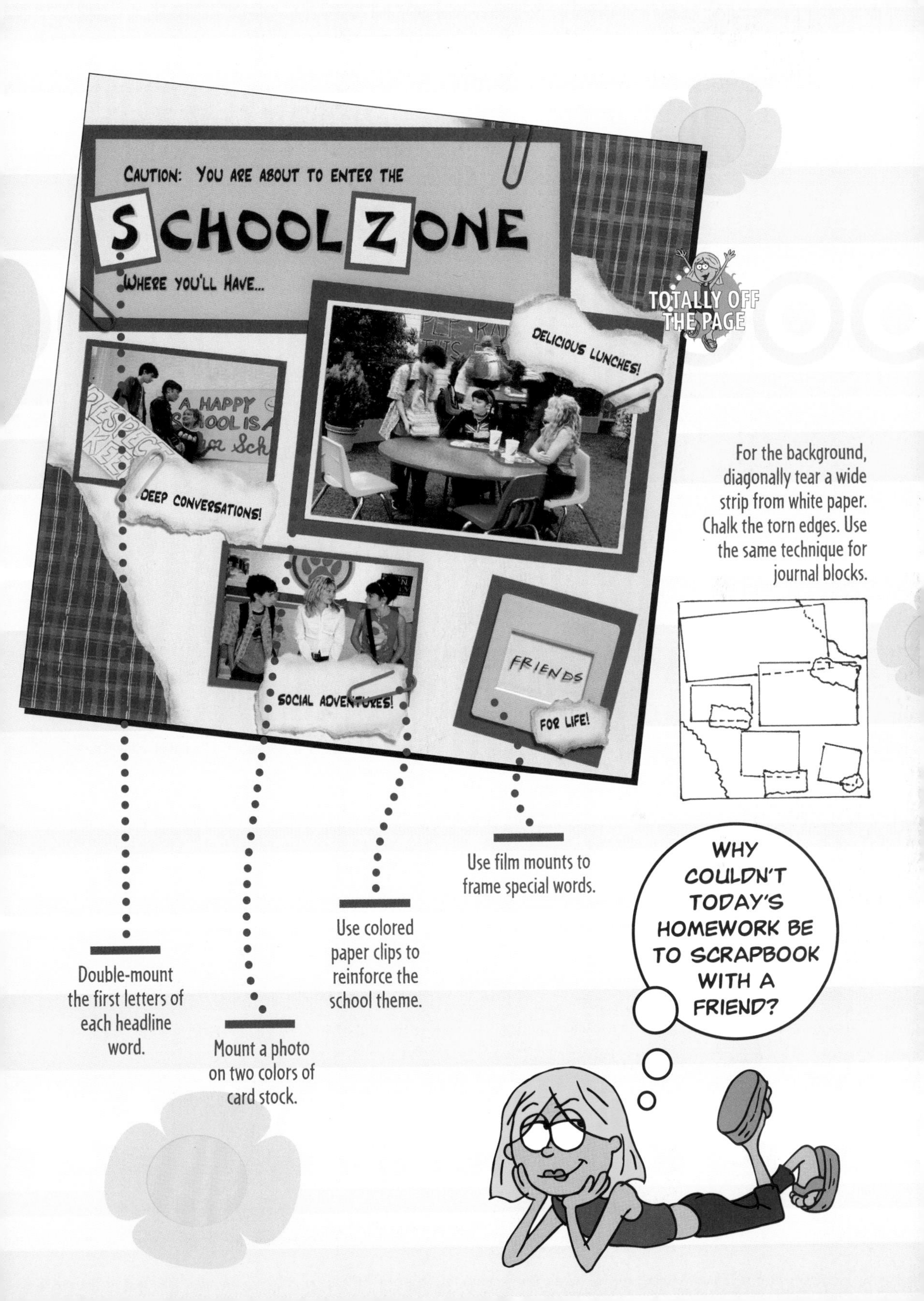
Caution: You are about to enter the
School Zone
Where you'll Have...
Deep Conversations!
Delicious Lunches!
Social Adventures!
Friends
For Life!
TOTALLY OFF THE PAGE
For the background, diagonally tear a wide strip from white paper. Chalk the torn edges. Use the same technique for journal blocks.
Use film mounts to frame special words.
Use colored paper clips to reinforce the school theme.
Double-mount the first letters of each headline word.
Mount a photo on two colors of card stock.
WHY COULDN'T TODAY'S HOMEWORK BE TO SCRAPBOOK WITH A FRIEND?

Miranda, Gordo and I just HAVE to eat while we solve the world's problems!

OK, let's face it, eating is one of life's major bonuses! Capture face-stuffing times with a scrapbook page that has all the right ingredients!

HERE'S ANOTHER COOL IDEA!

When you make scrapbook pages about your favorite foods, include these in the design: recipes, food wrappers (clean, of course!), menus, restaurant ads, close-up photos of the food, and color copies of tableware and dishes!

Turn the page to find out how to make each of these layouts.

TIME FOR A SNACK CONTINUED

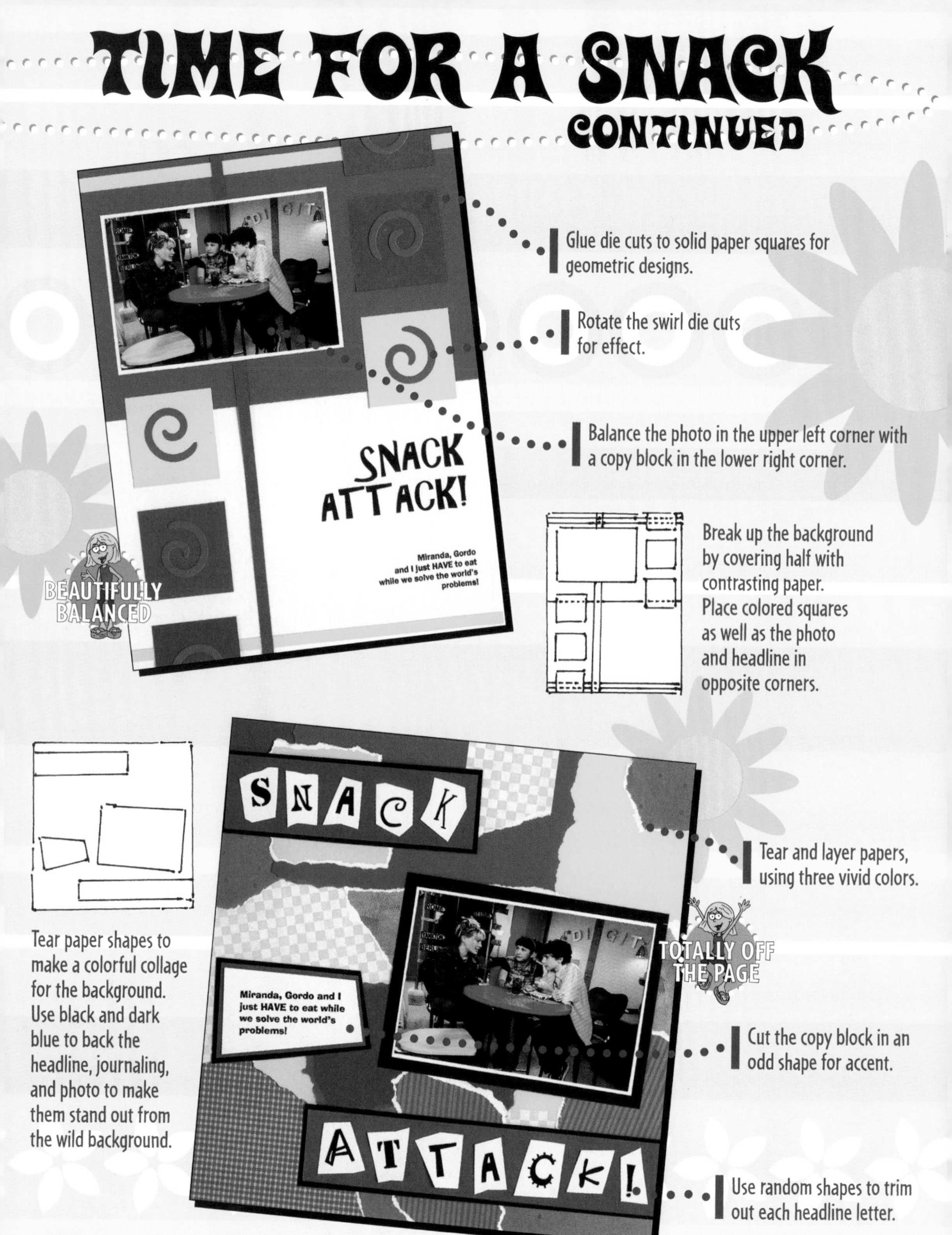

Glue die cuts to solid paper squares for geometric designs.

Rotate the swirl die cuts for effect.

Balance the photo in the upper left corner with a copy block in the lower right corner.

Break up the background by covering half with contrasting paper. Place colored squares as well as the photo and headline in opposite corners.

Tear and layer papers, using three vivid colors.

Tear paper shapes to make a colorful collage for the background. Use black and dark blue to back the headline, journaling, and photo to make them stand out from the wild background.

Cut the copy block in an odd shape for accent.

Use random shapes to trim out each headline letter.

Slightly tilted angles and irregular cuts add interest to this colorful page.

Two sizes of punches carry out the polka-dot theme on the blue and red paper.

Outline the journal block with a fine-line marker.

Cut paper strips for fries, photo frames, and page accents.

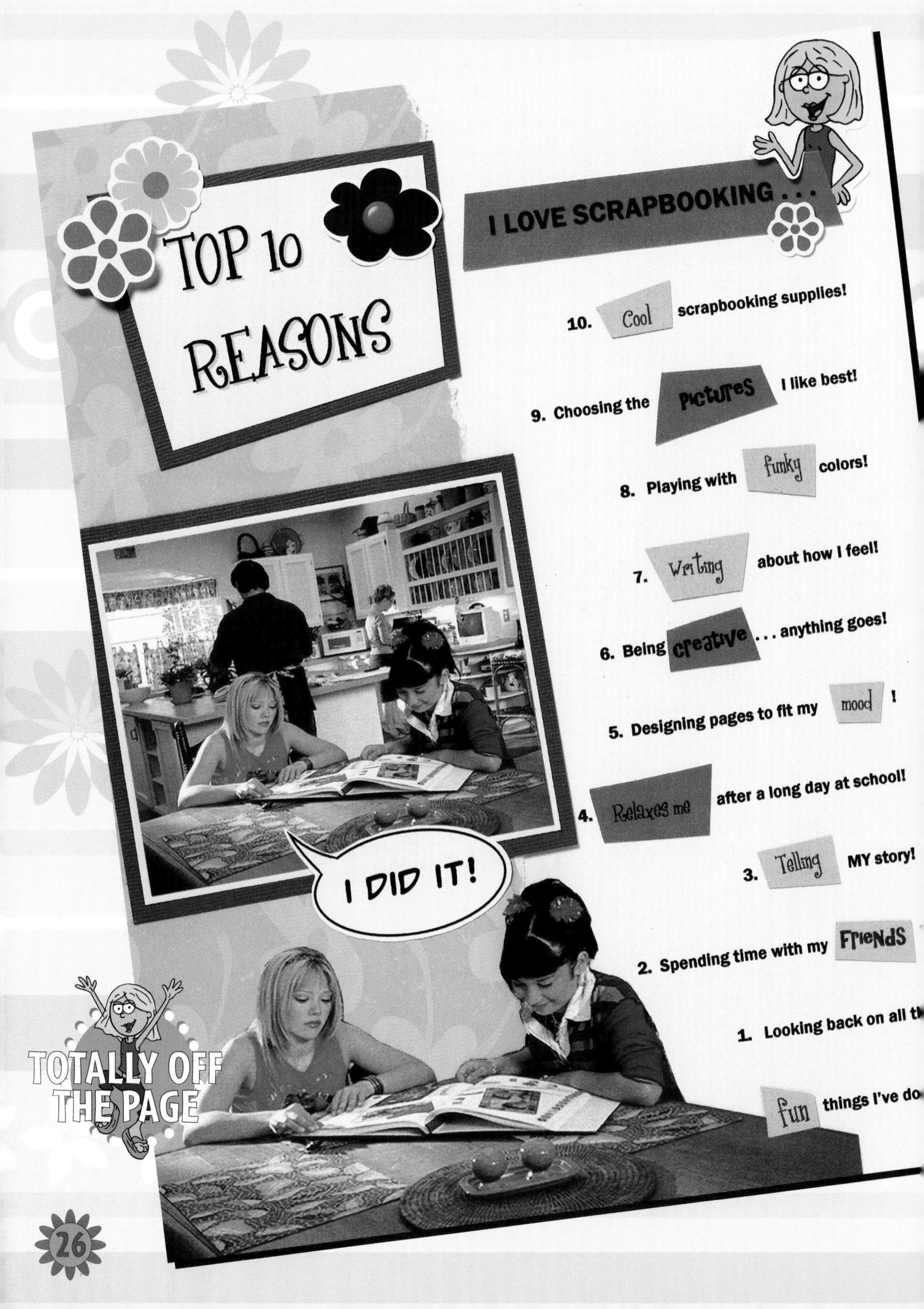
TOP 10 REASONS
I LOVE SCRAPBOOKING . . .
10. Cool scrapbooking supplies!
9. Choosing the Pictures I like best!
8. Playing with funky colors!
7. Writing about how I feel!
6. Being creative . . . anything goes!
5. Designing pages to fit my mood !
4. Relaxes me after a long day at school!
3. Telling MY story!
2. Spending time with my FRIENDS
1. Looking back on all
fun things I've
I DID IT!
TOTALLY OFF THE PAGE
26

BORN TO SCRAP

Making a scrapbook is tons of fun, and looking at it is even better! Here are some crafty ways to record you and your hobby.

IT'S ALL ABOUT YOU!

What's so cool about scrapbooking is that it is totally YOURS! It's a one-of-a-kind presentation, just like YOU!

Turn the page to find out how to make each of these layouts.

BORN TO SCRAP CONTINUED

TOP 10 REASONS

I LOVE SCRAPBOOKING . . .

10. Cool scrapbooking supplies!
9. Choosing the pictures I like best!
8. Playing with funky colors!
7. Writing about how I feel!
6. Being creative . . . anything goes!
5. Designing pages to fit my mood !
4. Relaxes me after a long day at school!
3. Telling MY story!
2. Spending time with my FrieNdS !
1. Looking back on all the fun things I've done!

I DID IT!

TOTALLY OFF THE PAGE

Add a brad to make the center of a Lizzie flower sticker.

Print words on two colors of paper and crop them into odd shapes.

Print the main journaling on white, leaving room for the cutout words.

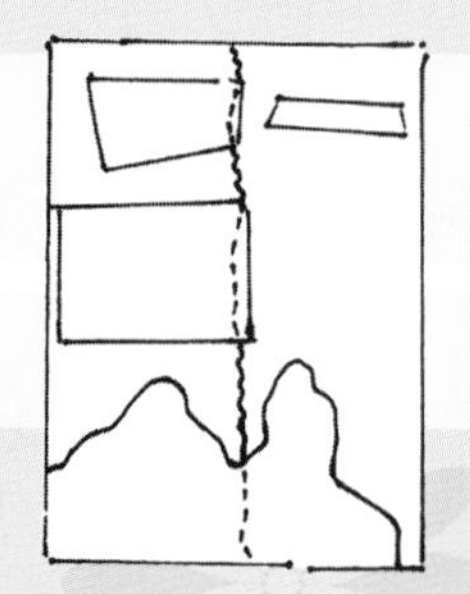

Tear a vertical strip from a subtle print paper for the left side. To anchor the page, glue a silhouetted photo at the bottom edge.

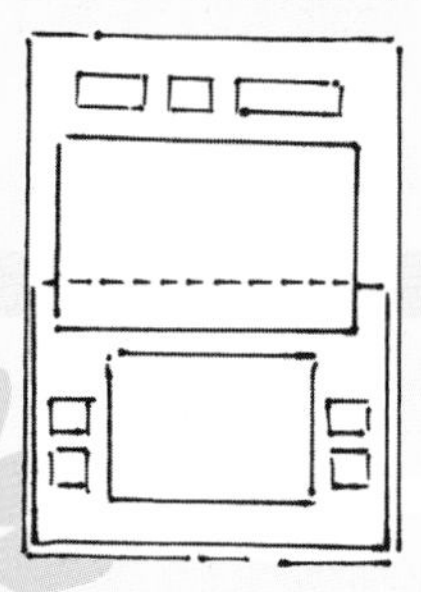

Cut a large rectangle from contrasting paper and adhere it to the bottom of the page, making narrow borders.

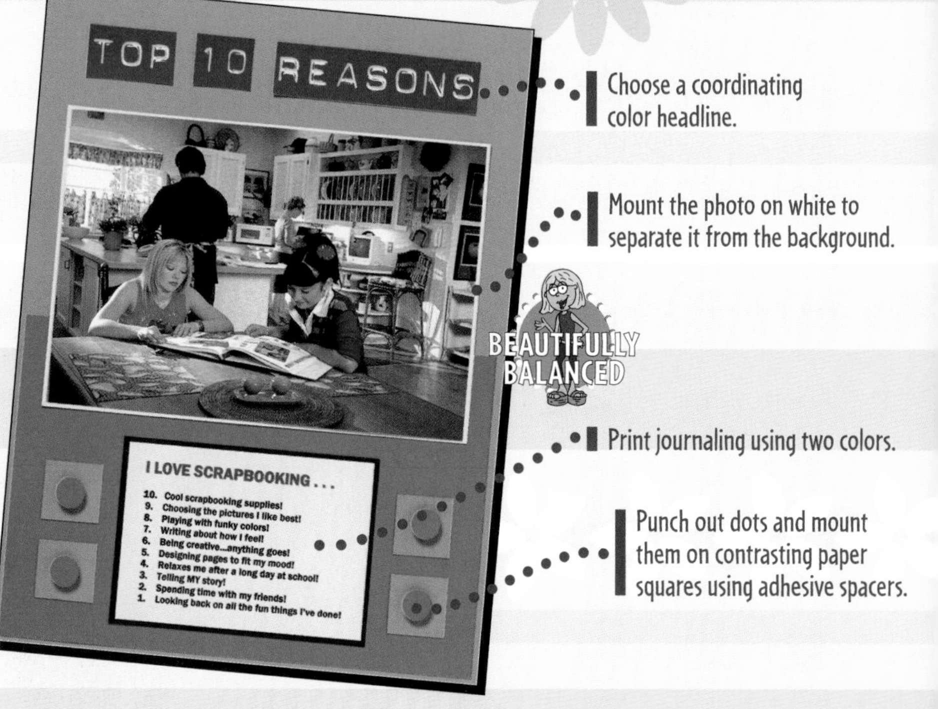

Choose a coordinating color headline.

Mount the photo on white to separate it from the background.

Print journaling using two colors.

Punch out dots and mount them on contrasting paper squares using adhesive spacers.

Cut three mottled papers for the background, allowing for narrow white borders to show.

Combine adhesive letters for an eclectic look.

Add borders to the top and bottom of color blocks.

Arrange stickers so some extend beyond the paper rectangles.

Choose stickers that represent the theme.

me
&
mom
One of
life's best
moments is
a quiet talk
with mom
and her hug.
TOTALLY OFF
THE PAGE

ME & MOM

Create a warmhearted page that's all about your relationship with your sweet and lovable, one and only mom.

IT'S ALL ABOUT YOU!!

Life is made up of a zillion different moments, and some of the most memorable are those spent with your mom! It's no wonder that the older girls get, the more they sometimes start acting like their mothers. That could be a really cool thing!

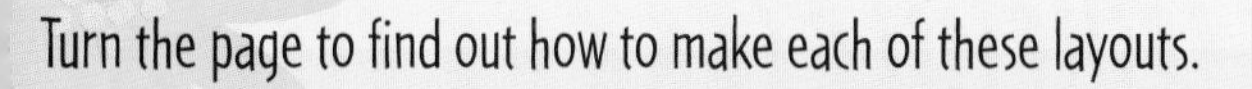
Turn the page to find out how to make each of these layouts.

ME & MOM CONTINUED

Thread cording through two eyelets and knot to secure.

Type a chunky headline and use the same font (only smaller) for the journaling.

Fill in open areas with large vellum stickers.

Trim the bottom of the journal box with decorative-edge scissors.

Angle a large contrasting piece of paper on the background. Arrange the copy and the photo below it straight; angle the photos on the left.

Choose solid color paper for the background that contrasts with the main color in the photo. Print the headline and caption on white, allowing space for the photo in the center.

Leave space between the headline and journaling to place the photo.

Center all of the type.

Randomly place vellum heart stickers on the page.

me and my
mom
COOL & CREATIVE
Enlarge a favorite photo and glue it to the left edge. Cover the entire page with vellum. Crop two photos the same size and print the headline to fit the upper left corner.
Align the two small photos and glue on the vellum layer.
Use two font sizes to print the headline.
Use eyelets to secure vellum to background card stock.
MY MOM LOOKS TOTALLY COOL–'CAUSE I HELP HER PICK OUT HER CLOTHES!

Painting
pots
COOL &
CREATIVE

THE ARTIST IN ME

Whether you like to paint, draw, sculpt, or craft with your mom, these creative layouts will inspire the artsy side of both of you!

BEAUTIFULLY BALANCED

TOTALLY OFF THE PAGE

IT'S ALL ABOUT YOU!

Everyone is good at something! Make a page about your latest sidewalk-chalk masterpiece or your last assignment for art class. Whatever you choose be sure to capture your artistic undertaking with YOUR style!

Turn the page to find out how to make each of these layouts.

THE ARTIST IN ME CONTINUED

Arrange sticker letters so a Lizzie sticker can "sit" on the word.

Cut paint blotches and drips from bright color paper.

Arrange the photo so the paper paint blotch cradles one corner.

Arrange and photocopy paintbrushes.

Surround the photo with the title lettering.

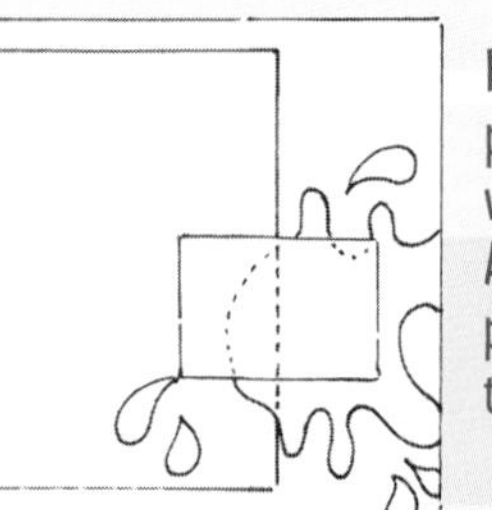

Photocopy paintbrushes on white paper. Adhere the photo to the background.

Center colored paper on black, leaving a ½-inch border. Mount the photo on black to make a window effect.

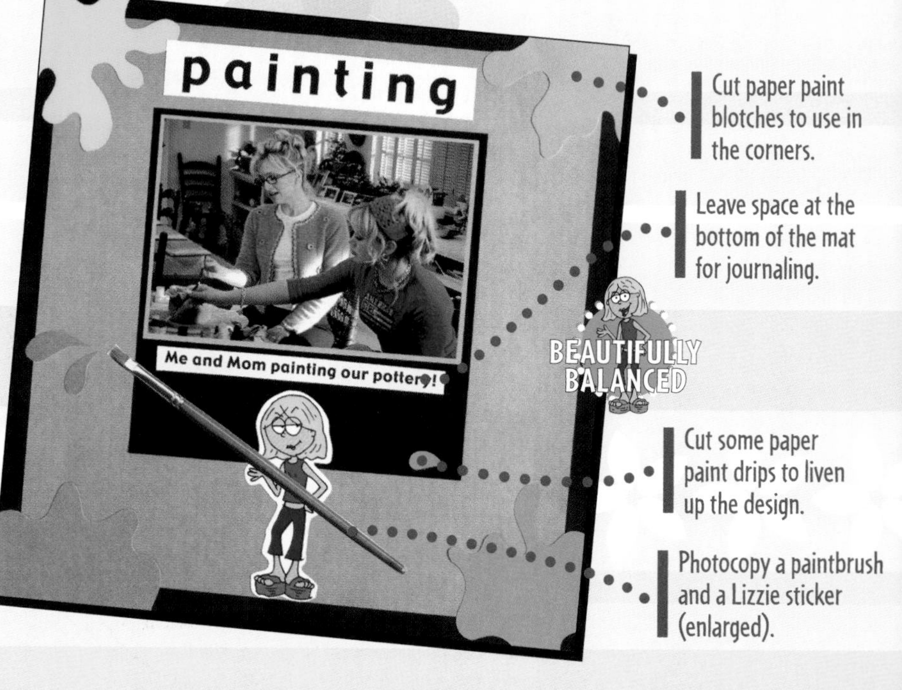

Cut paper paint blotches to use in the corners.

Leave space at the bottom of the mat for journaling.

Cut some paper paint drips to liven up the design.

Photocopy a paintbrush and a Lizzie sticker (enlarged).

TOTALLY OFF THE PAGE

Silhouette a photocopied group of paintbrushes to extend from one corner.

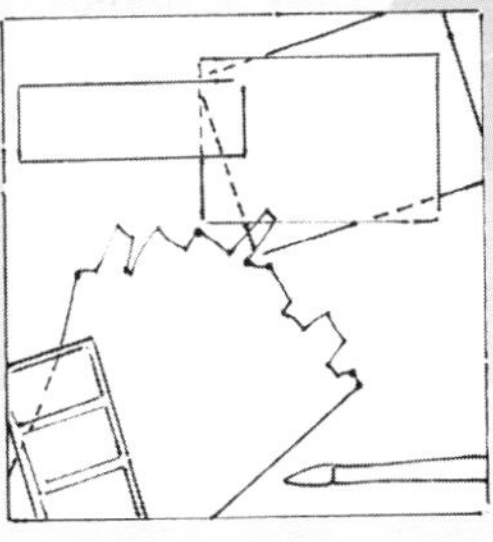

Group three small photos to extend off the page edge. Trim the photos even with the edge.

Place Lizzie stickers to stand, sit, or lie on the paper elements.

Glue a single brush near the bottom as a "bench" for a photocopied enlargement of a sticker.

Use a computer and printer to make your own conversation bubble.

I'D LOVE TO PAINT MY ROOM YELLOW— THEN ADD SOME FLOWERS, A FEW BUTTERFLIES...

KICKIN' BACK
GORDO
is such a
cool friend!
TOTALLY OFF
THE PAGE

FRIENDS RULE

Make a page (or twelve!) about your secret-keeping, fun-loving, always-there-for-you friend...your best buddy!

IT'S ALL ABOUT YOU!

Every time you start a new grade or a new activity, you're bound to add a new friend or two to your list. To personalize pages about these friendships, surround photos with such things as signatures, descriptive words, and the dates and details about how you met.

Turn the page to find out how to make each of these layouts.

FRIENDS RULE CONTINUED

TOTALLY OFF THE PAGE

Silhouette a smaller figure from a photo to "sit" on a larger one.

Add half circles by gluing flat sequins under the edge of the photo.

Align sticker dots to create a contemporary look.

Add detail with sticker strips.

Cut a small journal box into a paisley shape.

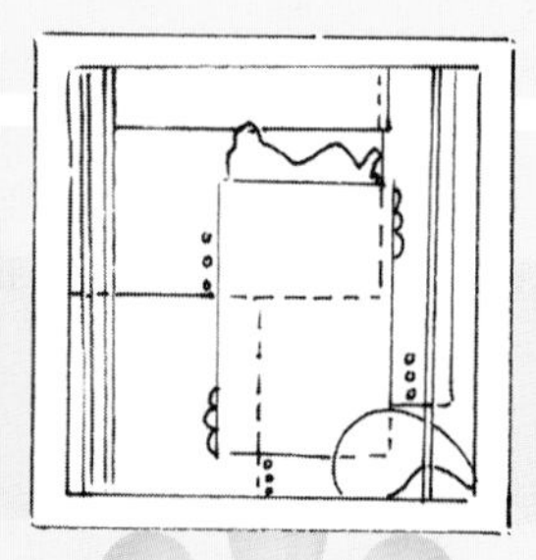

Use bold card stock rectangles on the background. For a 12-inch album, trim the page $^{3}/_{4}$ inch on each side and mount on a contrasting 12-inch square.

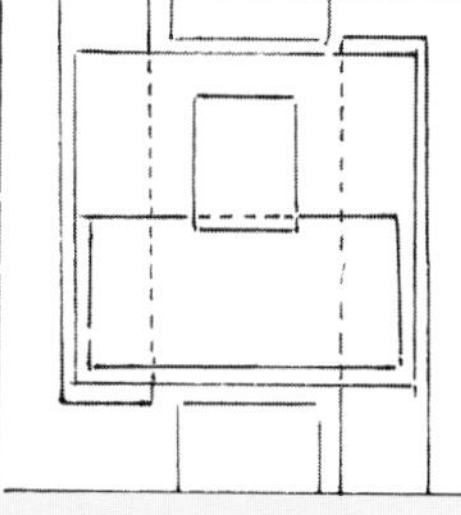

Overlap a small vertical photo over a larger horizontal one. Choose coordinating card stock to create the color-block background on black.

Draw a guide for stickers using disappearing ink.

Allow black borders around the center card stock pieces.

BEAUTIFULLY BALANCED

Cut the left and right color blocks the same size.

Save time using a background paper that's divided into color blocks and stitched together. Repeat the stitched zigzag using pinking shears to trim photos, the journal block, and details.

Trace around a drinking cup on the back of a photo and cut out with pinking shears.

Cut a strip from a leftover part of a photo.

Print the headline on a coordinating color of card stock.

Silhouette a small shape at the top of the photo to break into the headline block.

Awesome headlines!

Cut out these headlines to use on your scrapbook pages.

ST. LOUIS

Other ways to use your photos!

To use photos over and over again, make color photocopies in a variety of sizes. Then get ready to personalize your stuff!

- Decoupage photos on the cover of a scrapbook, album, or diary.
- Cut out a few photos, mount them on card stock, and glue magnets on the back. Then stick them on the fridge!
- Randomly glue photos on a wrapped birthday present. Glue a cutout to a plain piece of paper for the tag.
- Use photo transfer paper to put your face on shirts for friends.
- Cut photos into wide strips to use as bookmarks.
- Make a photo collage on a large sheet of paper to cover a book.
- Decoupage photos on a wastepaper basket, a pencil holder, or a lampshade.
- Cut out photos of family or friends in shapes to make holiday ornaments or a bedroom mobile.
- Mount scenic photos on plain note cards to make greeting cards.
- Make a collage of photos and laminate it for a place mat.
- Glue photos to storage containers that organize your stuff.

Seriously cool!
BEAUTIFULLY BALANCED

When you pose for family photos, make sure you get copies for your scrapbook.

COOL & CREATIVE

TOTALLY OFF THE PAGE

HERE'S ANOTHER COOL IDEA!

Keep a journal about your family history. Along with the usual stuff, like who married who, keep track of such fun things as favorite foods, pets, jobs, phobias, bad choices, embarrassing moments, favorite outfits, memorable gifts, and more—everything that makes your family one of a kind!

Turn the page to find out how to make each of these layouts.

MY FAMILY ROCKS CONTINUED

- Use decorative-edge scissors to cut corner strips.
- Use stickers from the back of this book to accent the page.
- Double-mount the photo, trimming the outer mat with decorative-edge scissors.
- Center an enlarged photo on the page.
- Center a sticker that sums up your family.

Seriously cool!

BEAUTIFULLY BALANCED

Use solid color card stock that coordinates with the photo and stickers.

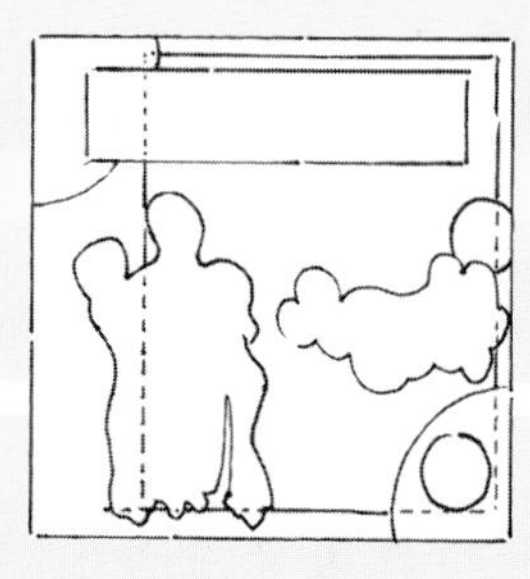

Spice up the background with circles cut from print papers. Layer and run some off the page for interest.

TOTALLY OFF THE PAGE

- With a computer, print a large headline.
- Use the stickers from the back of this book.
- Use $8^1/_2\times11$-inch print paper for the background.
- Use a circle cutter to make quick shapes.

COOL & CREATIVE

Mount the photo on a larger rectangle, such as the purple. Add a contrasting triangle at the top to create a house shape.

Use stickers from the back of this book. To make more, photocopy the stickers any size and cut out.

Crop your photo in a circle to place in the peak of the house.

Arrange star stickers to blend from one color to the next.

Use solid card stock to create a house design.

WHEN MY FAMILY TAKES A PHOTO, WE REALLY SAY "CHEESE"–HOW EMBARRASSING IS THAT?!

OUR DAY WITH CLAY
TOTALLY OFF THE PAGE

POTTERY 101

When you try something new and artistic, get some photos to relive the day!

COOL & CREATIVE

BEAUTIFULLY BALANCED

HERE'S ANOTHER COOL IDEA!

If you're like me, you love to roll up your sleeves, dive right in, and try something new. Take a look at each of the pages, above, and notice the photo of my hands around the clay. This close-up shot really adds to the page and says what it's all about–having fun with clay!

Turn the page to find out how to make each of these layouts.

POTTERY 101 CONTINUED

Use a circle cutter to cut the largest circle first, then cut a smaller one to make a ring.

Use a different font for each headline letter for a wild look.

Make several copies of one photo, crop them into circles, and place them around the large photo.

Make photocopied enlargements of stickers; cut out.

If an important photo isn't the best quality, use it small.

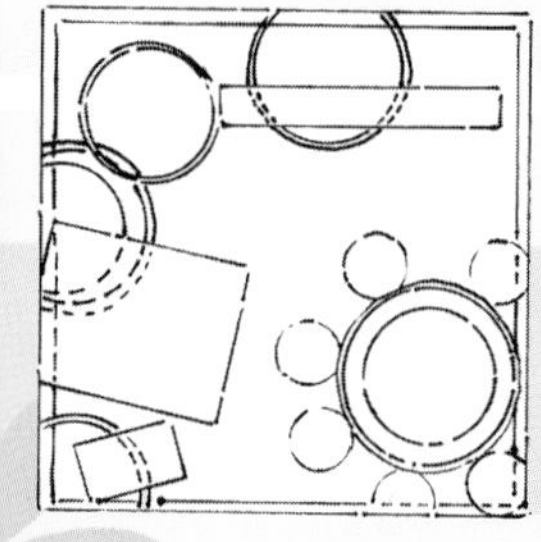

Use solid color papers for the background so the design doesn't get too busy. Crop most of the photos in circles, grouping some to organize the page.

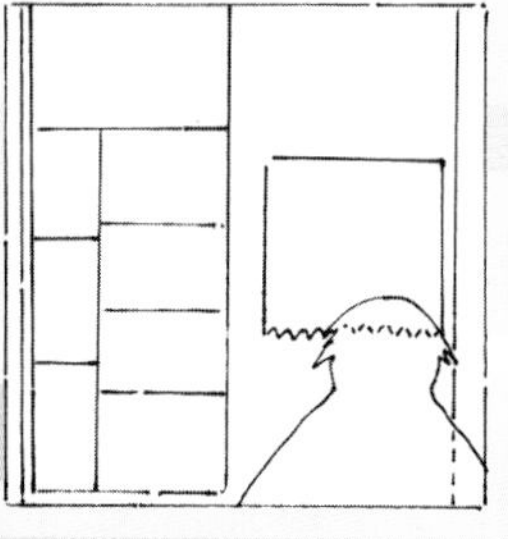

Layer a wide textured white paper strip on the black for the base of this page. Balance a group of photos with a larger silhouette.

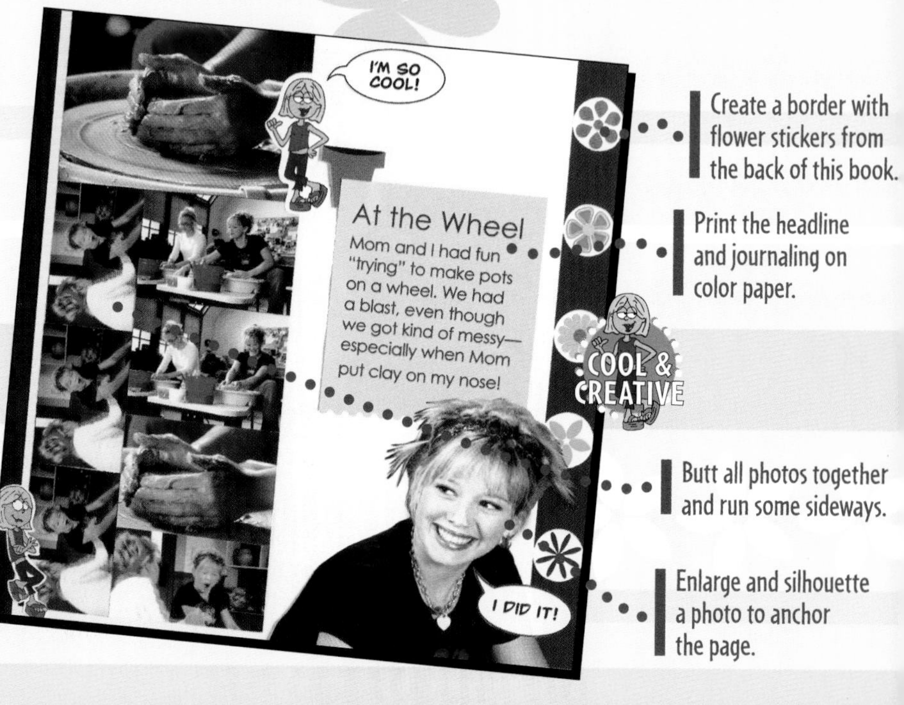

Create a border with flower stickers from the back of this book.

Print the headline and journaling on color paper.

Butt all photos together and run some sideways.

Enlarge and silhouette a photo to anchor the page.

THROWING POTS!
BEAUTIFULLY BALANCED
Crop all photos the same size and arrange in a grid pattern. Mat a small photo and place it in the center.
Double-mat the center photo to make it stand out.
To make a headline quickly, use alphabet stickers.
To eliminate photo mats, choose a background paper that contrasts with the photos.
Use stickers with adhesive spacers to lift them from the background.
I WONDER... IF I PUT CLAY ALL OVER MY FACE, WOULD IT BE CONSIDERED A FACIAL?

channel

surf·ing (sûr′fĭng) *n.*

1. The sport of riding on the crest or along the tunnel of a wave, especially while standing or lying on a surfboard. Also called **surfboarding**.
2. *Informal.* The activity of casually looking at something that offers numerous options, such as the Internet or television. 3. Something fun to do on the weekend!

Lizzie McGuire

snacks

cable

remote

episode

MOVIES

TOTALLY OFF THE PAGE

TIME FOR TV

OK, be honest! If your parents let you, you'd get a degree in TV! Show off your favorite TV watching spot or your most-watched shows on a cool page.

IT'S ALL ABOUT YOU!

What was your favorite TV show when you were four? Five? Six? Can't remember? That's why you should create this page! Use a piece of your TV section on the page or write out the names of old and new favorites so you'll know the hot shows of your time.

Turn the page to find out how to make each of these layouts.

TIME FOR TV CONTINUED

Use the TV section of a newspaper as part of the background.

Get out the dictionary to write a definition.

Use a film mount, beads, and wire to create a mini TV.

Include wrappers and color-coordinated stickers.

TOTALLY OFF THE PAGE

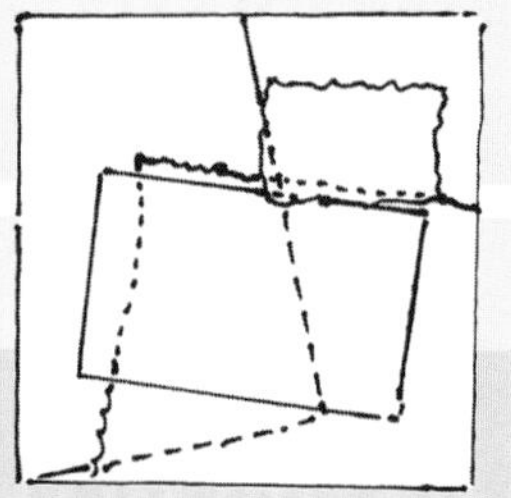

Layer papers and an unmounted photo on the background. Circle the photo with words, stickers, and (clean) wrappers.

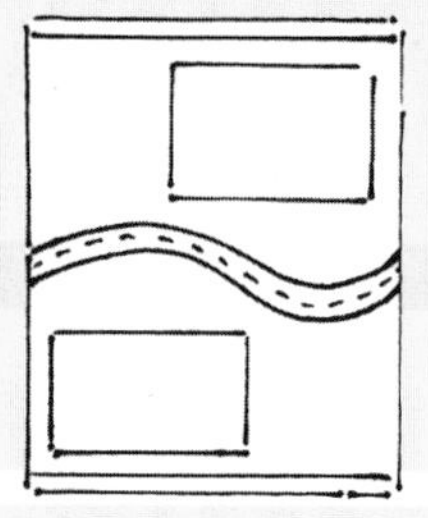

Divide the background using a wavy cut and three colors of card stock, keeping the brightest color in the center of the page.

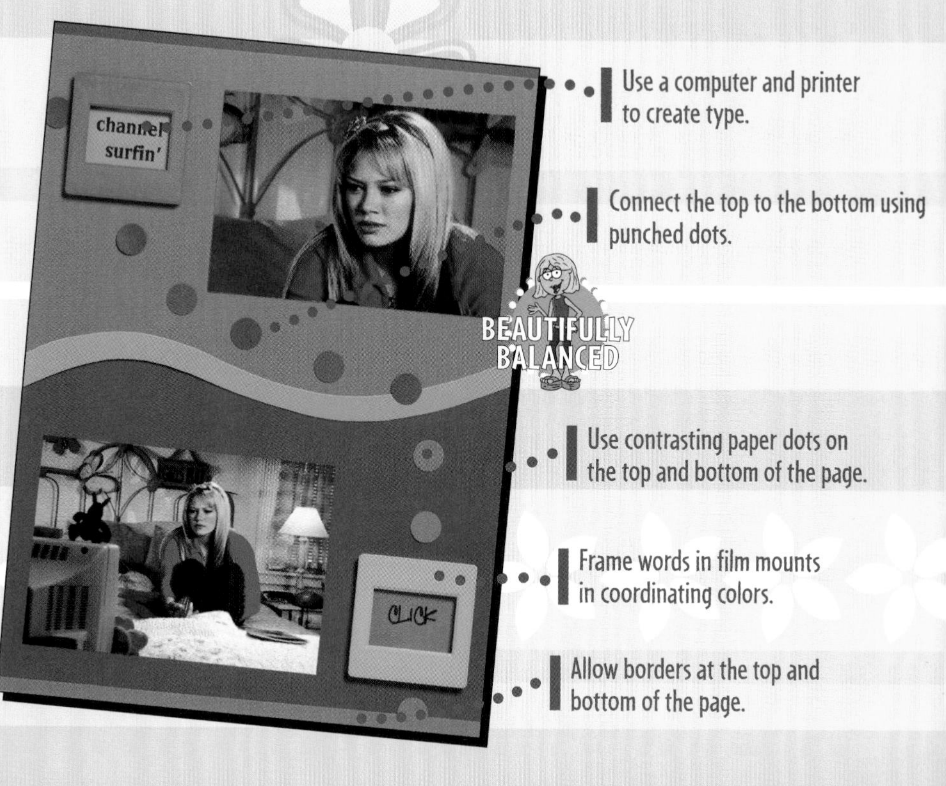

Use a computer and printer to create type.

Connect the top to the bottom using punched dots.

Use contrasting paper dots on the top and bottom of the page.

Frame words in film mounts in coordinating colors.

Allow borders at the top and bottom of the page.

Channel Surfin'
COOL & CREATIVE
CLICK
CLICK
Use white for the background and add two $1^1/_2$-inch-wide strips along the left side. Cut a patterned rectangle and place it on the right side.
Make butterflies from card stock and glitter.
Place contrasting strips side by side.
Arrange photos right up to the page edges.
HOMEWORK BEFORE TV— WHOSE BIG IDEA WAS THAT?!

curls
COOL &
CREATIVE

A GREAT HAIR DAY

When you have a look going that you really like, be sure someone takes a few photos!

IT'S ALL ABOUT YOU!

A hip, new haircut or a great outfit deserves a scrapbook page. Just three photos can tell the story.

Turn the page to find out how to make each of these layouts.

A GREAT HAIR DAY CONTINUED

Add alphabet stickers on a decorative tag for the headline.

Pick a background paper that has color and texture.

Soften the look with iridescent stickers.

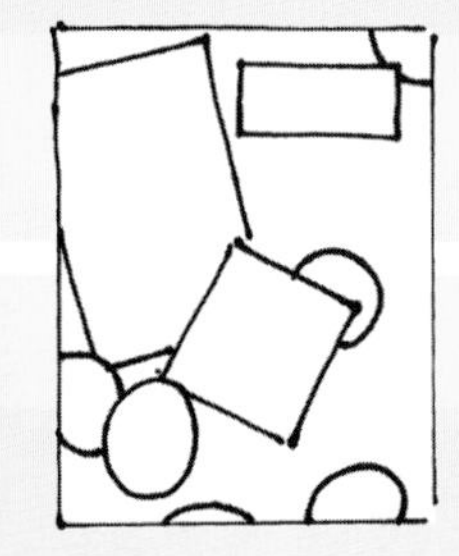

Overlap the photos in a pleasing arrangement. Add circles, a tag, and headline to complete the page.

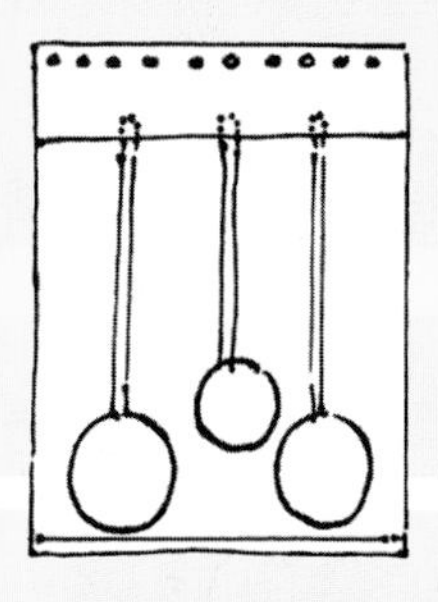

Cut four narrow and one wide paper strip. Punch holes across the top of the wide paper strip and back it with a contrasting piece of colored paper.

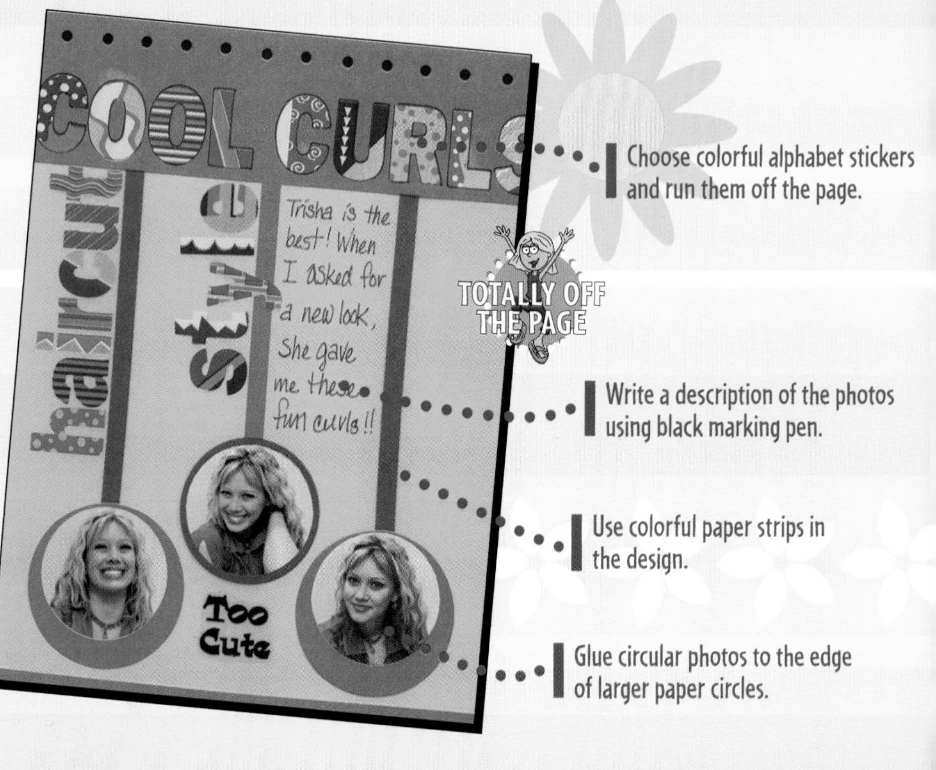

Choose colorful alphabet stickers and run them off the page.

Write a description of the photos using black marking pen.

Use colorful paper strips in the design.

Glue circular photos to the edge of larger paper circles.

Cut a rectangle from print paper for the background. Cut a narrow strip from the same paper to underline and trim the headline.

Cut out a design from print paper using decorative-edge scissors.

Use a circle cutter to cut two photos.

Draw a curved pencil line to guide your writing.

Silhouette a large photo and glue it to the bottom of the page.

School
DAZE
Going back to school this year was so fun! Miranda, Gordo, and I ended up in some of the same classes. It was great to see all of our friends again! We took these pictures during the first week of school...in the hallway, at my locker, in class, and at the bus stop.
SCHOOL BUS
STOP
905461
SCHOOL IS TOTALLY COOL!
Seriously cool!
BEAUTIFULLY BALANCED

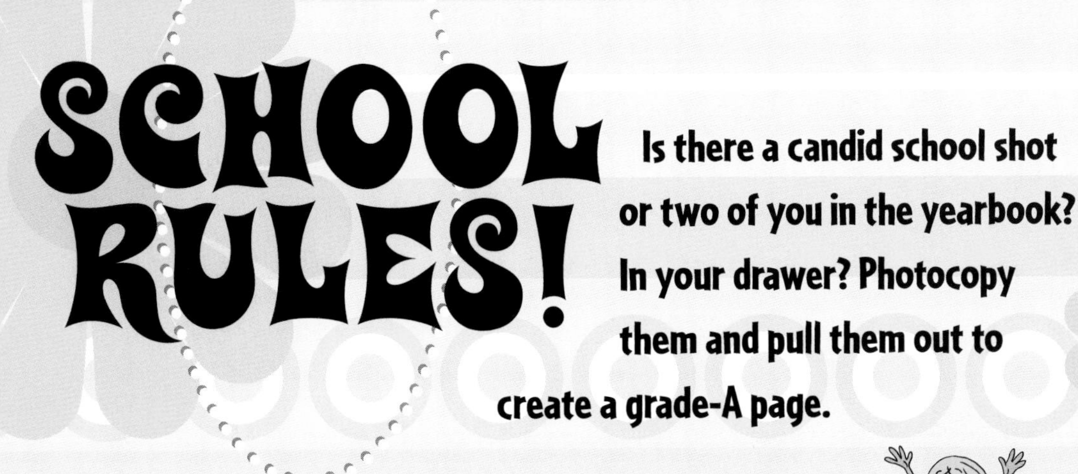

SCHOOL RULES!

Is there a candid school shot or two of you in the yearbook? In your drawer? Photocopy them and pull them out to create a grade-A page.

IT'S ALL ABOUT YOU!

Use your class picture each year to create a page all about your days as a student. Be sure to record the year and whatever else you have going on—cheerleading . . . science club . . . student council . . . band . . . volleyball . . . detention (NOT!).

Turn the page to find out how to make each of these layouts.

SCHOOL RULES! CONTINUED

- Use photos that tell your story about school.
- Use stickers from the back of this book for detail.
- Mount colorful card stock squares on white to create a background of quadrants.
- Balance the headline with an angled photo.
- Place an eyelet in each outside corner.

Use card stock squares to create four sections. Place photos in all of the squares, leaving room for the headline and journaling in the upper left section.

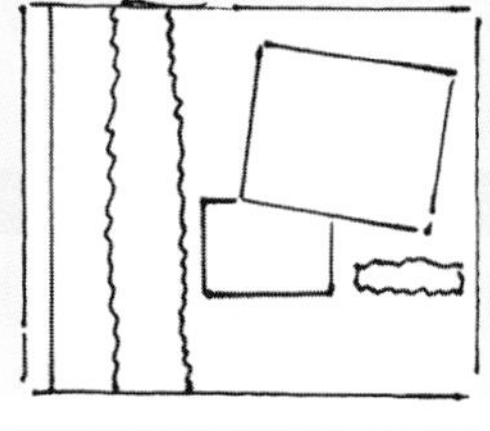

This interesting layout fits a horizontal $8^1/_2 \times 11$-inch album. Place torn papers and fibers at the left edge and fill the rest with photos, a headline, journaling, and flower stickers.

- Use adhesive spacers to raise some stickers from the page.
- Mount the photo on two papers, tearing the edge of the largest mat.
- Attach meaningful words using flower-shape eyelets.
- Print the headline and journaling on white card stock.

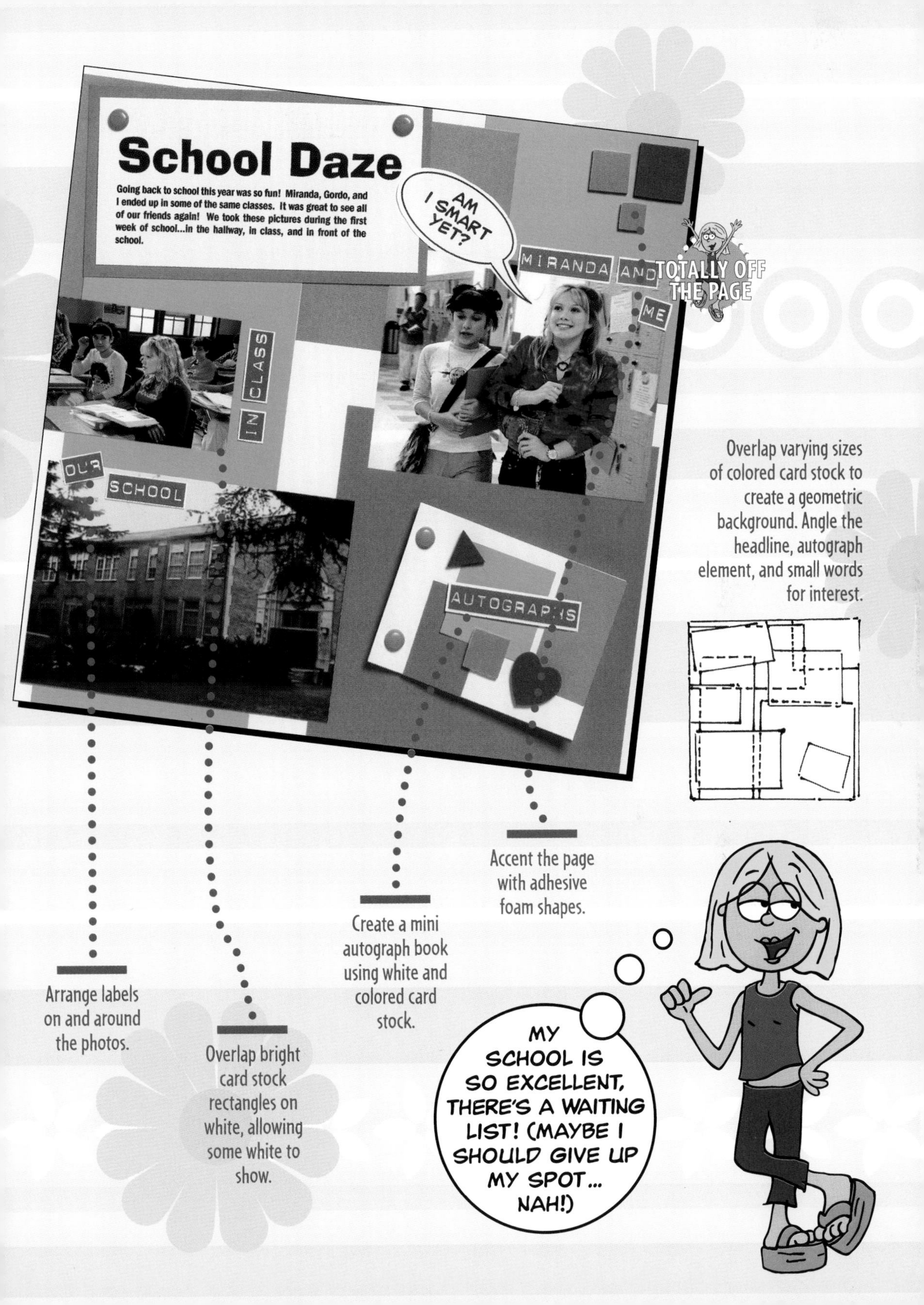

Overlap varying sizes of colored card stock to create a geometric background. Angle the headline, autograph element, and small words for interest.

Accent the page with adhesive foam shapes.

Create a mini autograph book using white and colored card stock.

Arrange labels on and around the photos.

Overlap bright card stock rectangles on white, allowing some white to show.

DREAMS
SECRET DREAMS
Your life is a journey
with dreams to pursue,
Discovering what
really matters to you,
For dreams are the voice
of your wisdom within
That whispers the way
each path you be
So whether you dream of true love or succe
of knowledge, or sharing the gifts you posse
Believe in your hopes, for as strange as it see
Your heart will find home if you follow your DREA
-author unkn
TOTALLY OFF THE PAGE

LIVE YOUR DREAM

Whatever you dream, dream BIG, and show your hopes and plans on a special scrapbook page.

IT'S ALL ABOUT YOU!

Do you dream of being a doctor? Would you like to travel to Africa and ride an elephant? Or do you want to be a singer who records songs? Wherever your heart leads you, remember your plans on a dreamy scrapbook page!

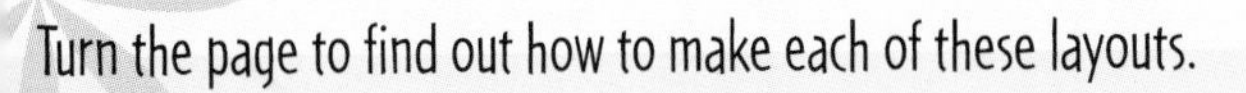
Turn the page to find out how to make each of these layouts.

LIVE YOUR DREAM CONTINUED

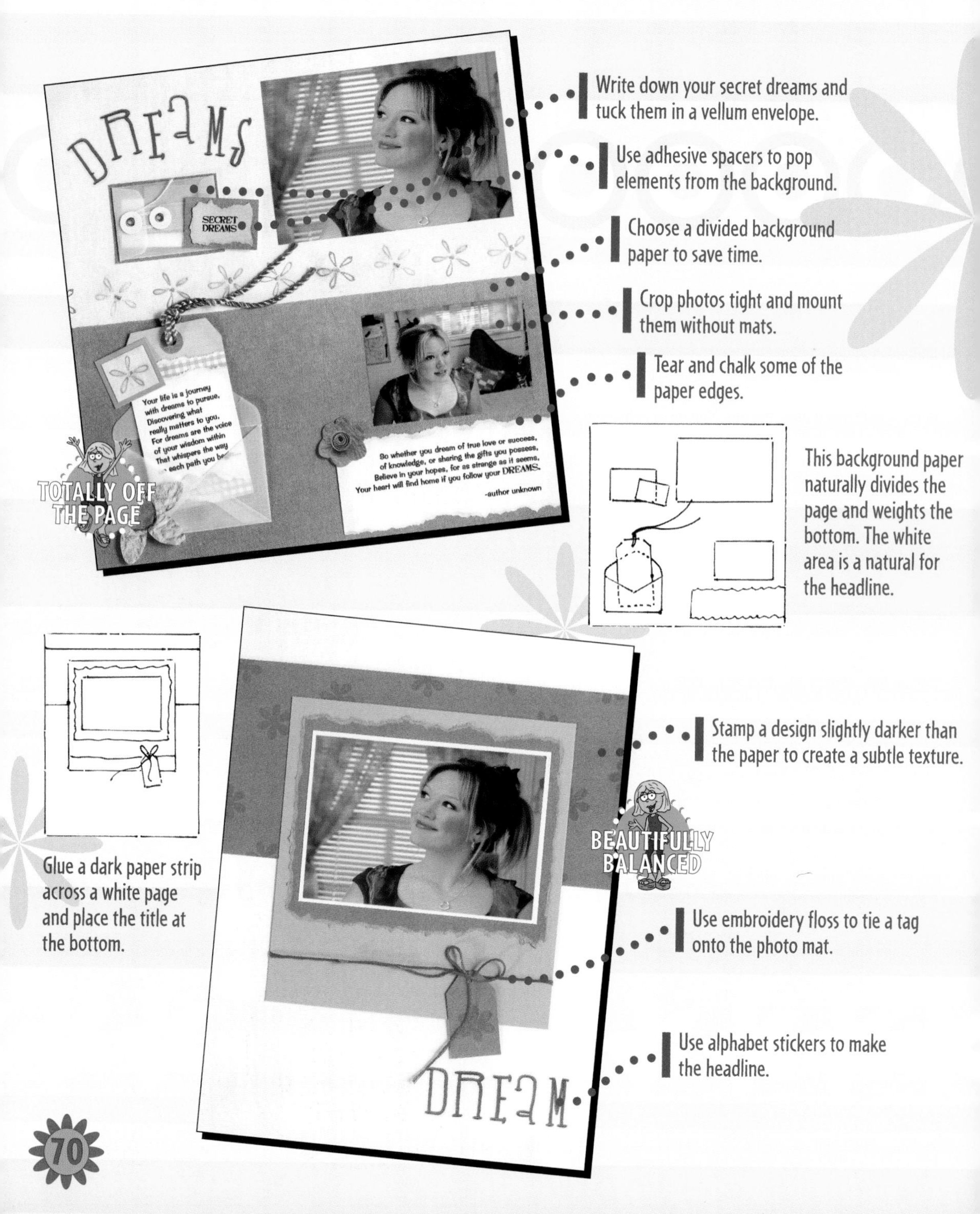

Write down your secret dreams and tuck them in a vellum envelope.

Use adhesive spacers to pop elements from the background.

Choose a divided background paper to save time.

Crop photos tight and mount them without mats.

Tear and chalk some of the paper edges.

This background paper naturally divides the page and weights the bottom. The white area is a natural for the headline.

Glue a dark paper strip across a white page and place the title at the bottom.

Stamp a design slightly darker than the paper to create a subtle texture.

Use embroidery floss to tie a tag onto the photo mat.

Use alphabet stickers to make the headline.

This is what DREAMS are made of....
COOL & CREATIVE
Secret Dreams
Place a patterned paper on a white background, leaving room at the top for the headline.
Use solid colors to mount photos.
Use beaded accents to add sparkle to the page.
Tie sparkly fiber through an eyelet on the tag.
Use a computer and printer for headlines.
A WEEKEND WITH NO HOMEWORK... I SAY, "LET'S SCRAP!"

CRAFTING PAGES

Born to Scrap 26-29
Pottery 101 52-55
The Artist in Me 34-37

DREAM PAGES

Live Your Dream....68-71

FAMILY PAGES

Good Ol' Mom 10-13
Me & Mom 30-33
My Family Rocks....48-51

FOOD PAGES

Time for a Snack....22-25

FRAMES

Circle motif....76
Floral 74
Square motif....80
Stripe....78

FRIEND PAGES

Friends Rule 38-41

HAIR PAGES

A Great Hair Day 60-63

Headlines....42
Lizzie Papers 73-80
Lizzie Photos....43-46
Lizzie Stickers ....back of book

PAPERS

Circle motif....75
Floral 73
Square motif....79
Stripe....77

PHONE PAGES

Hi, It's Just Me 14-17

SCHOOL PAGES

School is Cool....18-21
School Rules!....64-67

SCRAPBOOKING PAGES

Born to Scrap 26-29

TV PAGES

Time for TV....56-59

To use this paper as a photo border, use these lines as guides for trimming. You can also use the entire patterned page (on page 73) as scrapbook paper to "Lizzie-up" your own scrapbook pages.

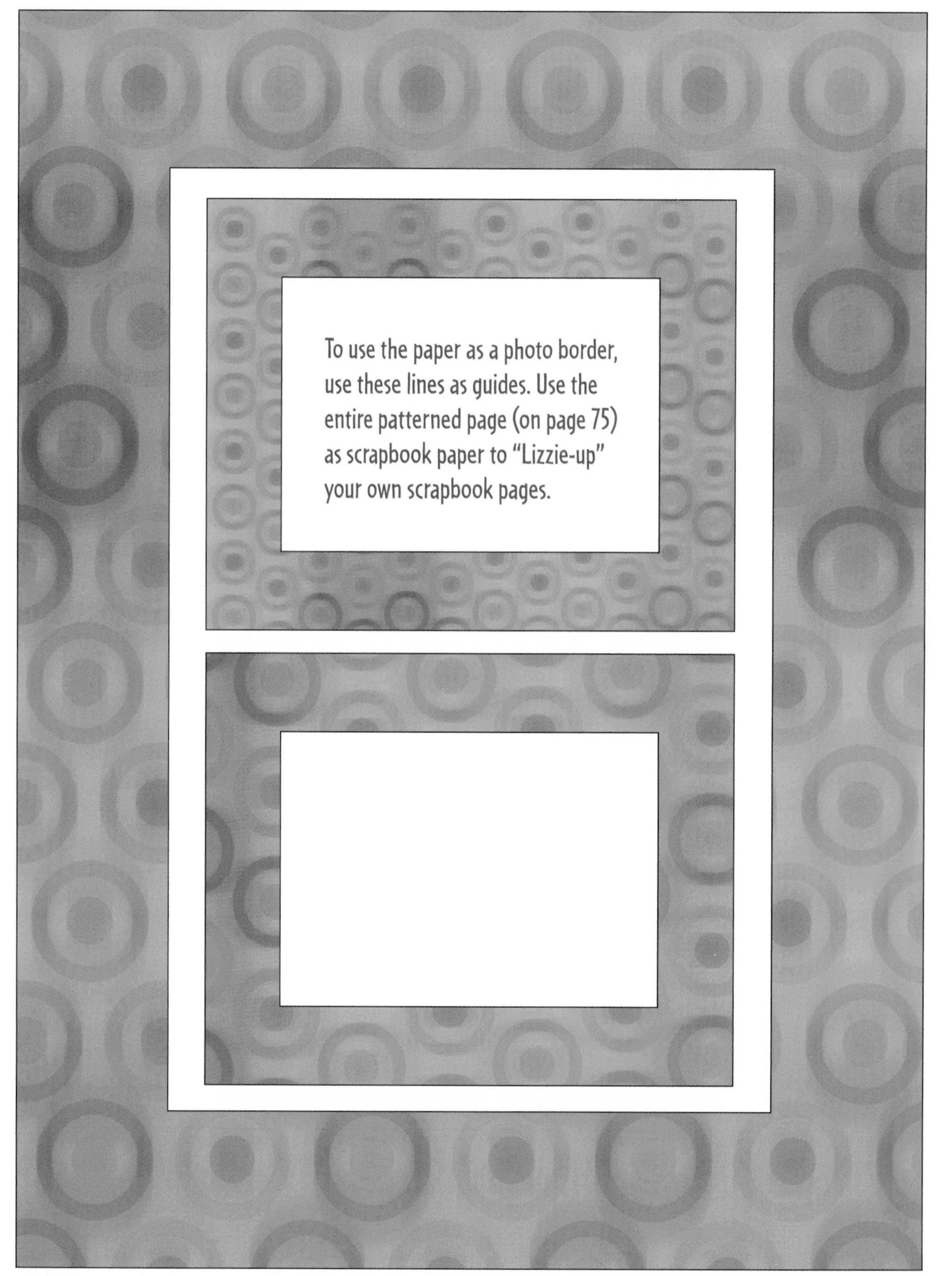
To use the paper as a photo border, use these lines as guides. Use the entire patterned page (on page 75) as scrapbook paper to "Lizzie-up" your own scrapbook pages.

To use the paper as a photo border, use these lines as guides. Use the entire patterned page (on page 77) as scrapbook paper to "Lizzie-up" your own scrapbook pages.

78

To use the paper as a photo border, use these lines as guides. Use the entire patterned page (on page 79) as scrapbook paper to "Lizzie-up" your own scrapbook pages.

80